MY MUM IS FANTASTIC

Nick Butterworth

WALKER BOOKS
AND SUBSIDIARIES
LONDON • BOSTON • SYDNEY

My mum is fantastic.

Warwickshire
County Council

0127186642

First published 1989 by Walker Books Ltd
87 Vauxhall Walk, London SE11 5HJ

This edition published 2001

4 6 8 10 9 7 5 3

This book has been typeset in Times

Printed in Hong Kong

British Library Cataloguing in Publication Data:
a catalogue record for this book is available from the British Library

ISBN 0-7445-8249-0

She's a
brilliant artist ...

and she can
balance on a
tightrope ...

It's great to have a mum like mine.

It's fantastic!

Nick Butterworth says of ***My Mum Is Fantastic***,
"I wonder how much time I spent as a boy singing the praises of my family. My grandpa could make *anything* out of *anything*. My gran was the best friend anyone could ever wish for. My dad was little short of Superman and my mum ... well, perhaps she actually *was* Wonderwoman! It's heartening to know that children feel the same today as I did then. Especially my own two!"

Nick Butterworth has worked as a graphic designer, television presenter, magazine editor and cartoon-strip illustrator, as well as producing numerous successful children's books. These include the Walker titles *My Dad Is Brilliant*, *My Grandpa Is Amazing*, *My Grandma Is Wonderful*, *Making Faces*, *Jack the Carpenter and His Friends* and *Jill the Farmer and Her Friends* as well as the bestselling *Percy the Park Keeper* series. He lives in Suffolk.

ISBN 0-7445-8248-2 (pb)

ISBN 0-7445-8250-4 (pb)

ISBN 0-7445-8251-2 (pb)